Sky Memories

Sky Memories

PAT BRISSON

PAINTINGS BY
WENDELL MINOR

❦ ❦ ❦ ❦

DELACORTE PRESS

Published by
Delacorte Press
a division of Random House, Inc.
1540 Broadway
New York, New York 10036

Text copyright © 1999 by Pat Brisson
Illustrations copyright © 1999 by Wendell Minor

Library of Congress Cataloging-in-Publication Data
Brisson, Pat.
    Sky memories / Pat Brisson ; illustrations by Wendell Minor.
        p.   cm.
    Summary: When ten-year-old Emily learns that her mother
has cancer, the two of them begin a ritual that will help Emily
remember her mother after she is dead.
    ISBN 0-385-32606-8
    [1. Mothers and daughters—Fiction.   2. Cancer—Fiction.
3. Grief—Fiction.]   I. Minor, Wendell, ill.   II. Title.
PZ7.B78046Sk   1999
[Fic]—dc21   98-38962
                                                                      CIP
                                                                        AC

The text of this book is set in 13-point Stempel Garamond.
Book design by Trish Parcell Watts
Manufactured in the United States of America
June 1999
10 9 8 7 6 5 4 3 2 1
BVG

In memory of all the mothers
who had to leave their children too soon;
and for their children—
may they find the strength, love, and courage to go on.
—P.B.

To the memory of Florence's mother, Etta.
—W.M.

The year before my mother died, we gathered sky memories. It began one day when I saw a car from Montana with "Big Sky" on the license plate.

"Is the sky bigger in Montana?" I asked my mother.

"Hmm," she said, thinking. "It's probably that they have fewer hills and buildings, so you can see more of it. But our sky's wonderful, too."

"It looks pretty regular to me," I said, looking up at it. "What's so wonderful about it?"

"It's wonderful because it's always changing. Sometimes it's beautiful-wonderful and sometimes it's scary-wonderful and sometimes, like now, it's just regular-wonderful."

I wasn't convinced.

"Do you know what we should do?" my mother asked. "We should gather sky memories. This one will be our first."

We drove to the park and walked out to the middle of the soccer field.

"Tell me what you see," my mother said.

"It's just grayish," I told her.

"Look harder," she said. "It's not *all* gray. Do you see how the sun shining behind those clouds makes them almost white? And look over there. . . ."

She pointed, and I saw a tiny patch of blue.

"My grandmother always told me that it was sure to be a nice day as long as I could find a patch of blue sky large enough to mend a Dutchman's breeches."

"What are breeches?" I asked.

"Breeches are pants that come down to just below the knee," she explained. "And I think there *is* enough blue sky to mend

those breeches, so I guess it's going to be a nice day. Now, try to notice everything, and when you're ready, we'll take a picture of it with our minds."

We stood there, holding hands and staring at the late-September sky. The wind blew our hair across our cheeks and stirred up the smell of damp earth and fallen leaves. Just then a flock of birds flew across the scene, as though we had planned it that way.

"When you think you're really seeing everything, squeeze my hand. That will be like the click of the camera."

I stood very still for about fifteen seconds; then I squeezed my mother's hand.

"Click!" we said together, and laughed.

"I love you, munchkin," she said.

"I love you, too, Mom," I told her.

She was right about that patch of blue sky: The day got nicer and nicer as it wore on.

That was my first sky memory, and I'll never forget it, because the very next day my mother found out she had cancer.

I was ten then and I didn't know very much about cancer, but I knew it was something really serious that people talked about in quiet voices and stopped talking about when kids came around.

"I'll do everything the doctor tells me to do," my mother said. "I'll be the very best patient he's ever had. Of course I'll get better, and to make doubly sure, we'll pray very hard that everything will be all right. Don't worry, Emily, I'll be fine."

I tried hard not to worry, and it helped that there was a lot of other stuff going on in my life just then. It was my first year in middle school, and I was still getting used to the new place. And Laura, my best friend since kindergarten, was in the other fifth-grade class. In all those years, we'd never been in separate classes before. I missed being able to trade looks with her when something funny happened.

I was also playing clarinet in the band that year. I had taken lessons for only a few months, so I wasn't as good as a lot of other kids. Practices went on forever, and I'd come home exhausted from concentrating so hard on my fingering and proper breathing. Then I'd practice some more at home. I knew Mom was sick, but sometimes I went days without thinking about it.

Then I'd hear her talking on the phone to Aunt Vicki about tests and second opinions and treatments, and I'd think that maybe things weren't going to turn out as well as my mother claimed they were.

It was at times like those that I wished I had a father. Another parent would have come in handy. But it had always been just me and my mom. Up until then, it had been enough.

O*ur next sky memory* was on Halloween night. Laura and I had dressed like ghosts, and my mother wore her necklace of jack-o'-lanterns that really lit up. It was the end of trick-or-treating and we were walking back home after dropping Laura at her house. I was wondering how many candy bars I'd be allowed to eat before bedtime, when my mom said, "Look at the sky!"

The moon was not quite full, but glowing, and long, narrow strips of clouds were moving quickly past it.

"Why do the clouds look black?" I asked her.

"Because the moon is so bright behind them and there's less light in front of them. Isn't it wonderful?" she asked.

"I think it's a little weird. Clouds are supposed to be white."

"It's weird-wonderful, then," my mother said. "What else do you see?"

"Only a few stars," I said. "And there's an airplane."

"Maybe it's a witch with a headlight on her broom," Mom said. "After all, it *is* Halloween."

"You're silly," I told her.

"Yes, I am, and you should be, too," she answered. "Shall we gather this sky memory?" she asked, holding out her hand to me.

I took her hand and looked at the sky—the thin, black clouds, the glowing moon, and the almost starless background. I thought of my mother's blinking jack-o'-lantern necklace and my bag of treats waiting to be explored. I squeezed her hand.

"Click!" we said together.

"I love you, my spooky goblin," Mom said.

"I love you, too, my silly mom."

When we got home, we went through my bag of treats together to make sure everything was safe. Then my mother said something that surprised me.

"So . . . how many treats do you think you should eat before bedtime?" she asked.

This was a bit of a trick question. If she'd asked how many I *wanted* to eat, I could have said fifty. But she'd asked how many I thought I *should* eat, so I had to come up with an answer that would make me seem mature. If I said a number that was too big, I'd sound like a little kid whose eyes were bigger than her belly, which is what my mother always said when I took more than I could eat. I thought for another minute.

"Four?" I asked with some hesitation.

My mother nodded. "That seems like a reasonable amount," she said.

I smiled to myself and felt very grown-up and responsible. It wasn't long before I realized how responsible I was going to have to be from then on.

That week my mother started treatments at the hospital. Aunt Vicki took her. The treatments made Mom tired and sick, but she said that just meant they were working. When I came home from school, I let myself into the house with my key, trying hard to be quiet and not wake her if she was sleeping.

If she was awake, she was often in the bathroom throwing up, or lying on the couch looking miserable. I would make her tea and bring her crackers when she felt too nauseated to eat anything else. And because even the smell of food made her feel sick, I ended up getting my own meals. This wasn't really a big deal. I usually just had cereal or a bagel for breakfast and took a sandwich for lunch. For dinner I heated up leftovers that Aunt Vicki brought us from the diner where she waitressed. Sometimes I made scrambled eggs or French toast.

I felt proud to be in charge of things, but scared, too. It just didn't seem right for me to be in charge, taking care of my mother. It was supposed to be the other way around.

The day after her first treatment, my mother overslept and didn't wake me up in time for school. She had already told the people at work that she wouldn't be in that week, so at least we weren't *both* in trouble. That day was the first time I'd ever been late for school in my life. Mom had told my teacher about having to start treatments, so he didn't get upset when I walked in late. He put his arm around my shoulder, gave me a little hug, and whispered, "Relax, Emily, we're just getting started. I hope everything went well yesterday for your mom."

That evening I asked Mom if I could keep the alarm clock in my room.

"I'm sorry, Emily, I must have forgotten to set it. Don't worry, it won't happen again," she told me.

But the next morning it *did* happen again. Luckily, I woke up twenty minutes before school started. I dressed in a rush, left without eating breakfast, and ran all the way, getting there just as the first bell rang. When I got home from school that afternoon, the clock was on the table next to my bed.

That night we had an early snow. It was wet and heavy and the big flakes melted when they hit the ground and made a slushy mess on the sidewalk. I turned off the lights in the living room and sat on the floor next to my mother, who was lying on the couch. We stared out the window together as the fat, white flakes fell from the sky and got caught in the glow of the streetlight. They fell

steadily for a long time, and I was sure we'd have a snow holiday the next day. My mother put her hand on my shoulder, and I reached up to touch her fingers.

"Click!" we said together.

"I love you so much, my Emily," my mother whispered.

"I love you, too, Mom," I answered.

I didn't have a snow holiday. Those snowflakes were beautiful, but they just didn't last.

$\mathcal{S}$*oon after that,* Aunt Vicki started coming by more often. She phoned every day with my wake-up call to make sure I was ready for school. She did our grocery shopping, and she took me to the Laundromat and helped me do the laundry.

"When is my mom going to get better?" I asked her one day as we were folding towels.

Aunt Vicki is always truthful with me. I knew I could trust her to tell me the truth even if it wasn't very good.

"Your mom is pretty sick," she said, "but the doctor said these treatments could help, so we'll have to wait and see, Em."

"Did the doctor say they *could* help or they *would* help?" I asked her.

Aunt Vicki sighed and stopped in mid-fold. "There's no guarantee with this sort of thing, Emily. Often the treatments do help, but sometimes they don't. We have to be patient and hope for the best." She hugged me to her, the half-folded towel warm and sweet-smelling against my cheek.

I didn't like not knowing what was going to happen with my mom, but at least I knew as much as anybody else. I tried to do what Aunt Vicki suggested: be patient and hope for the best. It wasn't easy.

$\mathcal{O}$*ver the next few weeks,* my mother lost almost all her hair. At first I didn't notice, but then one morning I found a bunch of it in the shower and I made a point to look at her more carefully. Sure enough, there were patches where I could see her scalp. I had never seen a bald woman before. I didn't know women *could* go bald.

"Mom, what's wrong with your hair?" I asked her. "Why is it all falling out?"

She sighed and ran her hand through it and came away with another handful.

"I guess I should have warned you," she said. "It's a reaction to the treatments. Don't worry, Emikins, it'll grow back."

But it was hard not to worry. If my mother was going to be all right, why did it seem as if she was always getting worse?

One day soon after that, Mom was well enough to drive. We were heading home from the grocery store around dinnertime. There's one point along the way where a cornfield stretches out to the left of the road. On the edge of the field is a row of trees. It was the end of November, and all the trees were bare of leaves: the setting sun shone through and lit up the trees from behind.

"Look at that," my mother said, pulling the car over to the side of the road. "Isn't it wonderful?"

I didn't think so. "The trees look like skeletons," I said. "You can see every one of their branches. They look so cold and alone."

"Oh, they don't look sad to me, Emily; they look strong. It's almost as if they're saying, 'Come on, Winter, give us your best shot! We can take it!'"

She reached across the seat for my hand.

"Let's gather a sky memory," she said.

Her voice sounded enthusiastic, but her hand was icy cold, and thinner than I remembered. I looked out the driver's window at that long line of tree skeletons, and in the corner of my eye was the back of my mother's head. I tried to see the strength my mother saw in those lonely-looking trees, but all I could think of was how she was losing all her hair.

I squeezed her hand.

"Click!" we said together.

That year at the Christmas concert, my mother was the only woman in the audience wearing a baseball cap. It was a fancy one Aunt Vicki had gotten for her—all covered with purple and silver sequins. From the stage I could look out at that crowd of people in the audience and find her in an instant; the sequins caught the light from one of the fire exit signs and sparkled in the darkness. I was embarrassed until Laura said she thought the cap was cool. It's funny sometimes what a difference one little comment can make.

In February Aunt Vicki moved in with us. She brought along her dog, Tipper, who looked fat and slow but had a mean bark whenever a stranger came to the door. This was a little scary for me, and for the first few days I was startled every time I got home and heard barking when I began to open the door. After a few days, though, Tipper and I got used to each other, and then the barking wasn't scary at all but actually made me feel safer.

Aunt Vicki bought a rollaway bed at a thrift shop, and it just fit in my bedroom once we moved my chest of drawers out into the hallway. When Aunt Vicki wasn't around, my mother suggested that I should offer to sleep on the rollaway and let Aunt Vicki sleep in my bed. I didn't like the idea of losing my bed, but I knew it was more than just a suggestion. My mother would always say things like "I think it would be a nice idea . . ." when what she really meant was "I want you to . . ."

So I did offer my bed to Aunt Vicki, and then I was sorry it hadn't been my own idea, because Aunt Vicki said, "Why, bless your sweet heart, Emily. I don't know how many nights these old bones could take on that rollaway." And because she was so grateful, she took me to Kmart and bought me a brand-new set of sheets with tiny pink roses all over them. I felt like a princess the first time I slept on them; I didn't want to shut the lights off, they looked so good.

Aunt Vicki worked the late shift at the

diner and would sometimes bring home the pieces of pie nobody bought. Then Tipper and I would have pie for breakfast. My favorite was lemon meringue, but Tipper liked apple the best. Aunt Vicki taught me things, too, like how to play poker and make brownies. Twice she let me wear her blue scarf, which she said matched my eyes perfectly.

For a while after Aunt Vicki came, it seemed as if my mother was getting better. She smiled more and didn't sleep as much. She made me breakfast in the morning. She went for walks with me and Tipper and played poker at the kitchen table with me and Aunt Vicki.

Except that she had lost a lot of weight and always wore a baseball cap, it seemed just like the old days before she had gotten sick.

One morning in March I woke up and found my mother in my room, looking out the window.

"Mom?" I asked, not quite sure whether I was really seeing her or just dreaming her. "What are you doing?"

She turned and, even though the room was dark, I could tell from her voice that she was smiling at me. "Oh, Emily," she whispered, since Aunt Vicki was sleeping soundly nearby. "Come look at the sky. The dawn is so red this morning. You know what that means, don't you?"

"Red sky in morning, sailors take warning," I recited as I crawled out of bed and went to stand by her. She put her arm around me and hugged me to her.

"But what are the sailors being warned about?" I asked.

"Storms ahead, I guess," Mom said. "Or maybe windy days that will toss their boats about. No more smooth sailing, at any rate."

I shivered. Mom rubbed my back and kissed the top of my head.

"Get dressed quickly, so you don't get cold. I'll go make you some hot chocolate."

"Wait!" I said, before she could leave. "First, a sky memory."

She smiled and took my hand. We stood together, looking out at the brightening sky, the neighborhood houses and trees outlined by the morning. Then Tipper came into the room and sniffed my bare feet with his cold, wet nose. It made me giggle. I squeezed my mother's hand.

"Click!" we said together.

"Now you get dressed, sweetie," my mom whispered.

I took one more look out the window,

thinking of sailors being tossed to and fro in their boats at sea; then I pulled on jeans and a sweater.

*M*om *got sicker* that spring and went into the hospital for two long weeks. Aunt Vicki switched with her friend Joan, a waitress on the morning shift at the diner, so that she could be home with me at night. We went to visit Mom every day when Aunt Vicki got home from work.

I hated everything about the hospital except that I got to see my mom. It was full of people rushing all over, pushing wheelchairs, dragging mops and buckets, moving beds on or off elevators. People came in and out of my mom's room all the time, and I never felt as if we had any privacy. Bells rang, televisions blared, voices called out over the loudspeakers, people dropped things right outside her door. And the smells—yuck! I tried not to breathe or see too much as we walked to Mom's room. The first day, I glanced into a room and saw an old man's bare backside as he turned over in bed. My face burned with embarrassment, and from then on I kept my eyes glued to the floor until I got to my mother's room.

My mother had a tube running into her

arm, and she was really weak. She had lost more weight, and when we walked the halls together, slowly and for a very short time, she leaned on my arm. She was so frail, it seemed that she could be blown right off her feet by a strong wind.

In the past when spring came, we had always made a game of watching for the first signs of forsythia. On our drives to the grocery store or Laundromat, we'd keep our eyes peeled for the bright yellow branches. And when we saw some, we'd yell, "Forsythia! Forsythia!" The trick was to be the first to spot it.

Then, when it seemed as if forsythia was blooming on every corner in town, we'd have a tea to celebrate. Mom had a yellow teapot, which she'd take down from the shelf over the refrigerator, and we'd get out the pretty cups and saucers she saved for special occasions. We'd buy fancy cookies (the kind Mom usually said were too expensive), and we'd put on lipstick and lots of jewelry, then drink our tea with our pinkies up, pretending to be la-di-da. Sometimes it was just me and Mom, but the year before, we had invited Aunt Vicki and Laura, too. After we had our tea and cookies, we played three games of Parcheesi.

The year Mom was sick, it was different. She had just come home from the hospital and hardly ever left the house, so I was with Aunt Vicki when I spotted forsythia for the first time. When I yelled, "Forsythia! Forsythia!" Aunt Vicki said, "Heavens, Emily! You scared me half to death!"

Later that day I told my mother about it. I was standing next to her bed, lining up all the round bottles of pills on her nightstand. Since most of them were pre-scriptions from the same pharmacy, they all looked the same, like soldiers in uni-form. I lined them up perfectly, using the edge of a book to make sure the line was exactly straight, then flicked each one over onto its back. Flick, flick, flick, flick—right down the row, each one falling over with a rattle and thud. Then I'd line them up perfectly again and start all over.

"Aunt Vicki got mad because I yelled so loud when I spotted the forsythia," I told Mom. "She said we were lucky she didn't drive us right off the road into a tree."

Mom just smiled. "You caught her off guard," she said. "Don't worry; I'm sure she wasn't really angry."

A few days later, Aunt Vicki brought home a big bouquet of forsythia that hadn't quite bloomed yet. She had gotten it from one of her customers at the diner, and she said if we put it in water, we could watch it start to flower.

Mom and I didn't take any drives to spot forsythia that year, but we did have the tea. Only that year it was Aunt Vicki who shopped for cookies, got down the teapot, and made the tea. Mom managed to drink her tea and eat a cookie, and she wore earrings and a long strand of pearls, but she was too tired to play Parcheesi, so Laura and I played by ourselves while Aunt Vicki read a book and Mom went to bed. It was nice, but it wasn't quite the same.

Through the spring, Mom got worse. She lost even more weight, and her face got so thin it made her teeth look too big for her head. Her hair was mostly gone, but there were wisps of it here and there that stuck out from her head and looked weird. She slept a lot, and when she moved, she held herself as if she hurt all over.

I didn't play softball that spring, even though Laura was on the team. Since Laura wasn't around to hang out with, I got into the habit of coming home from school and going right to my mother's room. I would lie down next to her and tell her about my day. We'd talk about funny things that had happened in school or other things I'd been thinking about. And we'd eat peppermints together.

My mom had taken to sucking on peppermints all day long. She said she remembered that when her grandmother was old and close to dying, she had really bad breath. As much as my mom loved her, she found it hard to be too close to her then because the smell of her grandmother's breath almost made her sick. She said she made up her mind then that she would never let that happen to her.

When my mother told me that story, I said, "Well, *you're* not really old and close to dying."

Mom smiled. "You're right, Em, I'm not really old, but . . ." Her voice trailed off to nothing then, and she sighed. "I guess I just like peppermints," she finally said.

One day in late May I started to talk about things I hoped we could do that summer. But my mother stopped me.

"Oh, sweetie," she said, brushing the hair out of my eyes. "You'll have to talk to Aunt Vicki about the summer." Her voice was just above a whisper, and something in it scared me. I felt as though all the air was being sucked from my lungs and I couldn't draw another breath.

"What do you mean?" I asked, dreading to hear what she would tell me.

She took my hand and looked at it for a minute before kissing it. "I'm so sorry, Em, but I'm dying. I don't think I'll be here this summer." There were tears in her eyes, and she looked sadder than I had ever seen her look before.

"Mom," I whispered, "I don't want you to die. I keep praying and praying that God will make you all better. Why doesn't God answer my prayers?"

"Oh, my sweet Emily," my mother said, hugging me to her and kissing me on the top of my head. "God *always* answers our prayers. It's just that sometimes He says no. And it's so hard for us to understand, because we don't know as much as God knows. It's like when you were little and asked for cookies to eat before dinner and I had to say no. It didn't mean I didn't love you. I answered you; it just wasn't the answer you wanted to hear."

"But this isn't something dumb like cookies before dinner!" I shouted. "This is about you not being here and me not knowing what I'll do without you! Sometimes I think you don't even care about leaving me. Sometimes I think you really *want* to die!"

My mother started to cry. But I was

angry at her for not wanting to get better, and I didn't say I was sorry. I wanted to run away from her, but I also wanted her to hug me again and tell me she was sorry, that she hadn't realized how important it was to me, that she would try harder and wouldn't leave me.

"Emily," she said, "more than anything in the world I want to be here for you. But I can't, Em. I'm dying, and there's nothing I can do to stop that from happening. I wish so much that there were. I'm sorry, Em. Please forgive me. Try to understand."

She closed her eyes and continued crying.

Until that moment I hadn't thought

my mother would really die. I knew she was sick, sicker than I'd ever seen anybody be, but I'd always thought she'd get better. Now I knew she wouldn't.

I lay down on the bed next to her and we both cried. She smoothed my hair with her fingers and wiped away my tears.

"Are you scared?" I asked her after a while.

"Scared of dying?" she asked.

I nodded.

She thought for a minute before answering.

"No," she said at last. "I always thought I would be, but now that it's near, no, I'm not afraid. I fought it as best

I could, Emily, but this cancer just won't give up and I can't fight anymore. I'm worn out and ready to just fall asleep."

We were quiet for a few more minutes, and then my mother asked, "Are *you* afraid?"

"Yes," I admitted. "I don't want you to leave me. I'll miss you so much I won't be able to stand it. What will I do without you, Mom? It won't be the same at all."

"No, it won't be the same, Em," she said. "But it will still be good. Aunt Vicki loves you very much, and she'll take good care of you as you're growing up. Aunt Vicki and I talked about it for a long time. She even took me to a lawyer so I could put it in my will. She'll be your legal guardian, which is the next best thing to being a parent.

"So even though things will be different, you'll still be with someone who loves you almost as much as I do. And you are a smart, strong, wonderful girl who will be able to handle whatever comes your way. Having you was the best thing I ever did, Emily. I am so proud of you."

She smiled and kissed me.

"Look outside," she said. "Look at the light."

It was that brief moment between day and evening when the very air seems to shine with a special light. The colors of things look just slightly more intense, almost magical.

"It's the gloaming," my mother said. "Isn't it wonderful? It only lasts a few minutes."

I reached for my mother's hand, so thin, so frail looking, and squeezed it gently.

"Click!" we said together.

"I love you, Mom," I whispered.

"I love you, too, my Emily," she said.

We watched as the colors lost their intensity and the sky darkened. I turned toward my mother and snuggled next to her. She put her arm around my shoulder

and I lay there quietly, listening to the sound of her breathing.

*O*n the June morning when my mother died, Aunt Vicki woke me before dawn.

"Emily," she said, shaking me gently, "come see your mother." I was still sleepy, but I could tell from Aunt Vicki's voice that she had been crying. She smoothed the hair back from my forehead and kissed me. "She's very weak," she told me.

I tiptoed into my mother's room and leaned over to give her a kiss.

She smiled the tiniest of smiles and touched my cheek.

"Oh, my Emily," she whispered, "I love you so much."

"I love you, too, Mom," I said, and even though I didn't mean to, I started to cry.

"Hold my hand," my mother said, and without needing to say so, we both looked out her bedroom window.

It was still dark, and a thin, sharp crescent moon hung in the sky.

"Look," I said, squinting to make sure of what I was seeing. "There's a star hanging right between the two points of the moon. It looks like the star is falling and the moon is getting ready to catch it."

I wiped my eyes, took a deep breath, and gently squeezed my mother's hand.

"Click!" I said. But my mother had died.

Through the long summer after my mother's death, I cried until I thought I would run out of tears, and I wondered if I could ever be happy again. Aunt Vicki talked to me a lot about my mother and how much she had loved me. Aunt Vicki told me that *she* loved me, too, and would be there to take care of me now, since my

mother couldn't. She told me that even though it didn't seem possible, it would stop hurting so much after a while.

There were days when I felt as if I couldn't get out of bed. I was still so tired when I woke up that it seemed as if my body was held to my mattress with sacks of sand. Then Aunt Vicki would bring me juice and cinnamon toast on a tray. She'd sit next to me while I ate and would brush the hair out of my eyes. She'd tell me stories of when she and my mom were growing up—silly stories that generally made me laugh but sometimes made me cry because I still missed my mom so much. If I cried, sometimes Aunt Vicki cried, too, and we'd hold on to each other as though my bed was a raft and we were afraid of falling off.

One day Aunt Vicki asked me if I wanted to move into Mom's bedroom, or if it would be okay if she did. She said it didn't make sense for both of us to be squeezed into my room when my mother's room was empty. I knew she was right, but I still hated the thought of either one of us taking over Mom's space. A part of me kept thinking that Mom might still somehow come back to us, but only if her room was there waiting for her. It was crazy, I know, but that's what it felt like.

I couldn't find the words to explain all this to Aunt Vicki, though. I just kept saying, "No, don't!" and "I can't! I just can't!"

"Oh, Emily," Aunt Vicki said, pulling me into a hug. "I know it's hard. We don't have to change things right away, but you think about it, okay?"

I did think about it. I went into Mom's room and lay on her bed, memorizing every crack in the ceiling. There were still bottles of pills on the nightstand. I carefully lined them up in a perfectly straight row along the edge of the table. I flicked the first one off the edge. It fell to the floor with a familiar rattle and thud. I flicked the next one harder and it fell farther from the table. The next one I batted with my hand and it flew halfway across the room. The last three I gathered up and threw with all my might at the far wall. The plastic containers shattered and pills flew all over the room. I burst into tears.

Tipper barked at the noise I was making and came running into the bedroom, growling. Aunt Vicki was close behind. "Emily, what's wrong?" she asked as she hurried in. But I didn't answer her. I was down on the floor scooping up handfuls of pills and throwing them at the wall.

"I hate them! I hate them!" I screamed as I kicked at the pills scattered all over the floor. "I hate these stupid pills! They didn't make my mother better! They didn't keep her from dying! What good were they? Stupid, stupid pills!"

I tried to bend down to pick up another handful to throw, but Aunt Vicki stopped me and pulled me into a hard hug. "I know, Em," she whispered into my hair. "I know it's a hard time for you. But we'll get through this. I promise." She sat me down on the edge of the bed and sat next to me, rocking me slowly.

Over the next few weeks, I went into my mother's bedroom almost every day. I looked through her belongings and made myself put things into two piles. One pile was stuff to go to the hospital thrift shop. I thought it would be impossible to get rid of my mom's things, but really it wasn't hard deciding to give away her shoes and socks and stuff like that. The things I wouldn't give away went into the other pile. That's where I put her sequined baseball cap and her favorite blue sweater and the bright yellow scarf she wore when she got dressed up. I put her watch and some jewelry in that pile, too, because I couldn't bear to wear them right then, but knew I might want to someday. This pile I put back in the bottom dresser drawer.

Whenever I opened the drawer I could smell my mother's perfume, and I imagined her rising up out of that dresser like the mist that comes out of Aladdin's lamp and materializing in front of me. Sometimes this made me feel sad because deep down I knew it would never happen. But other times it made me feel happy because smelling her things made her seem to be there with me in a special way.

Eventually I had cleared enough space that I could move my stuff into my mother's room. Aunt Vicki had said she would move in there, if I preferred that, but since I'd spent all that time memorizing the ceiling, I figured I might as well stay there. Besides, I had gotten more used to it by then. We gave the rollaway bed to the thrift shop, too, and Aunt Vicki said the place felt so big, it was almost as if we had moved into a mansion. Aunt Vicki has a vivid imagination. That's one of the things I like best about her.

Laura and I spent almost every day together that summer. Sometimes we baby-sat for her little brother, Jeffrey, while her mom ran errands. Jeffrey was two and always made me laugh. Laura said that was because I didn't live with him. She said he wasn't as cute as everybody thought he was if you had to live with him. Maybe, but I liked the way I didn't have to think about serious stuff when I was around Jeffrey. I could just laugh and have fun and not think about missing my mother.

A lot of the kids I knew seemed embarrassed to be around me, as if they didn't know what to say or how to treat me. But Laura wasn't like that. She treated me the same as always. We still made jokes about stupid stuff the way we always had. We spent a lot of time playing five hundred rummy, and we rode our bikes to the library at least once a week and read our way through about a hundred books.

I liked the way Laura would say, out of the clear blue, things like "Remember the time your mom helped us make caramel apples?" or "Remember the time I slept over and your mom stayed up until one in the morning playing Monopoly with us?" Once when she said something like that, it made me cry. It wasn't that the memory was sad; it was a good memory. The sad part was realizing that there wouldn't be any more times with my mom ever again. That thought—the never-again part—was just too much to handle, and it made me cry. "I miss her," I said. "I miss her and I miss her and then I miss her some more."

Then Laura cried with me. "I know,"

she said. "I liked your mom a lot and I miss her, too." Laura and my mom used to talk and tell each other stories. Laura said sometimes it was easier for her to talk to my mother than it was to talk to her own. So I knew Laura was telling the truth about missing her, and that made me feel a little less alone.

The hardest times were at night. I would think about my mother as I lay in bed waiting to fall asleep. The more tired I was, the more I cried. I tried to do it softly so that Aunt Vicki wouldn't hear. It wasn't just that I didn't want to make her sad. Sometimes I wanted to be alone with my memories. But at other times, the crying was too much for me, and I needed Aunt Vicki to hold me and tell me it was going to be all right. We would get through it together. We would be okay.

Aunt Vicki was always there for me. She held me when I woke in the middle of the night. She hardly ever fought back when I got mad and yelled at her. She went on long walks with me and Tipper, took me and Laura bowling, and taught me how to make spaghetti and meatballs. I started to feel as if maybe I would survive this.

One night in late September, when I was in bed but not yet asleep, I realized that I hadn't thought about my mother for the whole day. At first I felt guilty, but then I realized it wasn't that I had stopped loving her, it was just that it had stopped hurting so much.

I got out of bed to kneel at the open window, and saw a moonless sky filled with stars. I could almost hear my mother saying, "Isn't it wonderful?"

I watched the sky for a few more minutes, until goose bumps rose on my arms. Then I whispered, "Click!" to the cool, damp air, went back to bed, and fell asleep.

About the Author

PAT BRISSON grew up in Woodbridge, New Jersey. She received a bachelor's degree and a Master of Library Science degree from Rutgers University and now works as a reference librarian. The author of ten children's books, she lives in Phillipsburg, New Jersey, with her husband, Emil, and their four sons.

About the Illustrator

WENDELL MINOR is an acclaimed painter who has illustrated numerous picture books and has created jacket paintings for countless adult and children's novels. His award-winning paintings have been exhibited throughout the United States. Born in Aurora, Illinois, he graduated from the Ringling School of Art and Design in Sarasota, Florida. He and his wife, Florence, live in Washington, Connecticut.